What do you do when your *mystery* is missing?

"Wait!" Kyle said. He pointed to Orson's bag. "Is that a secret spy kit?"

Orson nodded.

"Does it come with the Secret Spy Vanishing Ink Pen?" Kyle asked excitedly.

"Yeah," Orson said. "But I gave it to Nancy to use on her case."

Nancy's mouth dropped open. Orson's pen had vanishing ink?

"What?" Nancy cried. She opened her notebook and let out a gasp. The pages of her case were totally blank!

Oh, no! Nancy thought. *My Mystery of the Missing Hat—is missing!*

The Nancy Drew Notebooks

Available from Simon & Schuster

THE NANCY DREW NOTEBOOKS®

#52

Big Worry in Wonderland

CAROLYN KEENE
ILLUSTRATED BY JAN NAIMO JONES

Aladdin Paperbacks
New York London Toronto Sydney Singapore

This book is a work of fiction. Any references to historical events, real people, or real locales are used fictitiously. Other names, characters, places, and incidents are the product of the author's imagination, and any resemblance to actual events or locales or persons, living or dead, is entirely coincidental.

First Aladdin Paperbacks edition February 2003

Copyright © 2003 by Simon & Schuster, Inc.

ALADDIN PAPERBACKS
An imprint of Simon & Schuster
Children's Publishing Division
1230 Avenue of the Americas
New York, NY 10020

The text of this book was set in Excelsior.

Printed in the United States of America
10 9 8 7 6 5 4 3 2 1

Library of Congress Control Number 2002109950

ISBN 0-689-85428-5

Big Worry in Wonderland

1

Big Hat, Big Mouth!

Who in the world am I?" eight-year-old Bess Marvin asked in school. "That's the great puzzle!"

George Fayne rolled her dark eyes. "Duh!" she said. "You're my cousin, Bess!"

Eight-year-old Nancy Drew smiled at her two best friends. "Bess is just saying her lines, George," she said.

"That's right!" Bess said. Her blond ponytail bounced as she nodded. "The class play is almost a week away and I'm playing Alice in Wonderland!"

"I know!" George joked. "You've been

reminding us for the last three weeks!"

Bess placed her hands on her hips. "Well, at least I'm not playing a worm!"

"I'm a *caterpillar!*" George corrected. She stuck her chin up into the air. "And I get to blow a bubble pipe!"

Nancy giggled. Sometimes she couldn't believe Bess and George were cousins. They were as different as—worms and caterpillars!

"Just think!" George said. "Today is the first day we get to practice the play on a real stage!"

Nancy was happy to be playing the smiling Cheshire Cat, even though her cheeks were sore from so much grinning!

"I hope I remember my lines," Nancy said. "And to grin!"

"If you forget to smile," Bess said, "just remember the time the class gerbil crawled into Brenda's backpack."

Nancy giggled. Brenda Carlton was the snootiest girl in their third-grade class. Some people called her Miss Snooty Pants!

"Off with her head! Off with her head!"

Brenda shouted her lines as she walked up and down the auditorium's aisle.

"Why is she the Queen of Hearts?" George asked. "She's already a princess!"

"I know something you don't know," Bess said in a singsong voice. "Brenda is having a party on Saturday!"

"Why?" Nancy asked.

"To celebrate her part in the play," Bess said. "The part of the Queen!"

"I hope we're invited!" Nancy said. "Brenda has the bestest parties!"

"Even if she *is* snooty!" George said.

Bess's blue eyes suddenly opened wide. She pointed over Nancy's shoulder.

"Look!" she gasped.

Nancy spun around. Their classmate Orson Wong was wearing a big green top hat—with a red brim and a yellow polka-dotted hatband.

"Wow!" Nancy gasped. "That hat is tremendous!"

"What do you expect the Mad Hatter to wear?" Orson asked. "A beanie?"

Nancy and her classmates surrounded

Orson. Their teacher, Mrs. Reynolds, walked over and smiled.

"So that's the hat you told me about, Orson," Mrs. Reynolds said. "It's perfect for the Mad Hatter."

"My mom bought it at Sid's Novelty Shop," Orson said proudly. "The same place where I buy my Squishy, Squirty Heads!"

Yuck! Nancy thought. Orson was always sneaking those little rubber toy heads into school. They were as ugly as could be. And they squirted water when he squeezed them!

"Mrs. Reynolds is right!" Brenda said. She smiled as she gazed at Orson's hat. "That hat is totally *perfect!*"

"Too weird," Bess whispered to Nancy. "That hat isn't Brenda's style!"

Mrs. Reynolds called for attention. "Before we rehearse our play," she said, "I have a big surprise."

Nancy gave a little jump. She loved surprises. What could it be?

Mrs. Reynolds climbed a small staircase up onto the stage. She pulled a cord, and the curtain swished to the side.

4

"Awesome!" George gasped.

Nancy brushed aside her strawberry blond bangs, and stared at the stage. It was decorated with fake trees, rocks, flowers, and a table set up for a tea party!

"It's wonderful!" Nancy gasped.

"No, it's not," Bess giggled. "It's Wonder-*land*!"

Just then a man with wavy brown hair peeked out from behind a fake tree.

Who's that? Nancy wondered.

"Boys and girls, this is my good friend Troy Marvello," Mrs. Reynolds said. "He decorates the windows at Casey's Department Store. And he's decorating the set for *Alice in Wonderland*."

Troy smiled at the kids. But when he saw Orson his eyes popped wide open.

"What's the matter?" Orson asked. "Is my nose running?"

Troy pointed at Orson's hat and smiled. "That's it! That's the hat I was looking for!" he exclaimed. "For my new spring window at Casey's!"

"Orson!" Mrs. Reynolds smiled. "Wouldn't

it be nice to have your hat in the display window of Casey's Department Store?"

"Sorry!" Orson said firmly. "But this was the last hat at Sid's."

"I'll give you five pounds of jelly beans for that hat!" Troy blurted. "You do like jelly beans, don't you?"

"Sure," Orson said. He stuck his chin out. "But I like my hat more!"

"As you can see," Mrs. Reynolds sighed, "Orson really wants his hat."

"Well, so do I," Troy said. He stared at the hat as he walked away.

Wow! Nancy thought. Troy really wanted that hat.

"Okay, kids," Mrs. Reynolds announced. "The first scene we'll rehearse will be the Mad Hatter's tea party!"

Nancy wasn't in the tea party scene. So she took a seat next to George and watched.

"What do you like better, Nancy?" George whispered. "Being in a class play or solving a mystery?"

"Hmm," Nancy said with a smile. "I'll have to think about that one!"

Nancy was the best detective at Carl Sandburg Elementary School. She even had her own blue detective notebook where she wrote down all of her suspects and clues.

Nancy turned her eyes back to the stage. Orson sat at the head of the Mad Hatter's table. Next to him sat Kyle, who was playing the March Hare. Next to Kyle sat Molly, who was playing the Dormouse.

"No room! No room!" the three shouted when Bess, as Alice, walked to the table.

Alice placed her hands on her hips. "There's plenty of room!" she argued.

"Why is a raven like a writing desk?" the Mad Hatter quizzed Alice.

"I'm glad they've begun asking riddles," Alice said. "I believe I can guess that!"

Yes! Nancy cheered to herself. *Bess is remembering all of her lines!*

Next it was the March Hare's turn to speak. Kyle began his lines: "Do you mean you can find out the answer to—OWWWWWW!"

Nancy jumped in her seat. Onstage Orson

had turned around so suddenly that his hat had whacked Kyle right in the nose!

"He can't do that to me!" Kyle said, rubbing his nose. "I'm the March Hare!"

"It's not March, it's February!" Orson joked. He then pulled out a Squishy, Squirty Head. Molly ducked just as Orson squirted Kyle!

"Here we go again!" Nancy sighed. Orson was a good actor—but a major pest!

Mrs. Reynolds marched onto the stage. "There will be no arguing!" she scolded the boys. "And no Squishy, Squirty Heads!"

"Sorry." Orson sighed as he stuffed the rubber head into his pocket.

The rest of the afternoon seemed to fly by as everyone practiced their lines.

"I did it!" Nancy cheered after school. "I knew all my lines by heart!"

"And you didn't miss a grin!" George said as they filed out of the school.

Suddenly Nancy felt someone tap her on the shoulder. It was Brenda standing behind her.

"Hi, Brenda," Nancy said.

"Hi," Brenda said. "I'm having a party on Saturday. You three are invited."

"Neat!" Nancy exclaimed.

"Thanks, Brenda!" Bess said.

"It's at two o'clock sharp," Brenda said as she pulled three invitations from her backpack. "And everyone has to wear something special—"

"What should we wear?" George joked. "Snooty pants?"

There was total silence.

Brenda's face turned tomato-red. Her eyes burned as she glared at George.

Oh, no! Nancy thought. *What was George thinking?*

"Very funny, Georgia Fayne," Brenda snapped. "Just for that—*none* of you are invited!"

2

Follow That Script!

It was just a joke!" George told Nancy. "And I did tell Brenda I was sorry!"

"I guess some jokes aren't funny," Nancy said. "Especially when they're about yourself."

"Me and my big mouth!" George said.

Nancy was sad about the party, but glad it was a mild afternoon for February.

Nancy, George, Bess, and many of their classmates stayed in the schoolyard to play. Nancy and George ran to the swings. Bess stood to the side, reading her script.

As Nancy swung back and forth she

could see Molly and Amara jumping rope. Orson and Andrew were playing kick-ball.

But where was Orson's hat?

Just then Nancy spotted the hat. It was on top of Orson's backpack. And under the biggest tree in the schoolyard.

Nancy was about to look away when someone peeked out from behind the tree. It was Kyle Leddington. He eyed Orson's hat with a sneaky look on his face.

Then—*WHOOSH!* A huge gust of wind blew across the schoolyard.

"Nancy! George!" Bess shouted. "The wind just blew my script away!"

Nancy and George jumped off their swings and ran to Bess.

"Look!" Bess cried.

Nancy looked to see where Bess was pointing. Her *Alice in Wonderland* script was tumbling across the schoolyard!

"We have to catch it!" Bess wailed. "I drew little pink hearts next to all my lines."

The three friends grabbed their backpacks. They chased the script throughout the busy schoolyard. The wind carried it past the seesaws and monkey bars. Then it lifted the script into the air and dumped it over a row of bushes.

Nancy and her friends squeezed through the bushes. She found Bess's runaway script—in the hands of Lonny and Lenny Wong!

Lonny and Lenny were Orson's six-year-old twin brothers. They were pests, too—and double the trouble!

"That's mine, thanks," Bess said, holding out her hand.

"Nuh-uh!" Lonny said. "We won't give it back until you watch some of our magic tricks!"

"Magic tricks?" Nancy repeated.

"We want to be magicians!" Lenny explained. "Just like Orson once was."

"Before he became a famous actor!" Lonny said proudly.

Nancy rolled her eyes. Orson used to practice magic. When he wasn't practicing mischief!

"Okay," Nancy said. She held up her finger. "But just *one* trick."

The twins jumped up and down.

"Watch closely," Lonny announced. He pulled a candy gummy worm from his pocket. "Now you see it . . ."

Lenny opened his mouth wide. Lonny popped the gummy worm right in.

"Now you don't!" Lonny declared.

"That's it?" George demanded while Lenny chewed. "*That's* your trick?"

"Yup," Lenny said with his mouth full. "But don't tell our mom. We're not allowed to eat candy after school."

"And you shouldn't be allowed to take other people's things," Nancy said. She reached out and snatched back the script.

"Some magicians!" George snorted. "Come back when you can pull a rabbit from a hat!"

The twins' eyes lit up.

"Timmy Pendergast has a pet rabbit!" Lenny declared.

"Let's go for it!" Lonny cheered.

As the twins high-fived, the girls squeezed through the bushes.

"I'm so glad my script is back!" Bess said, hugging the papers to her chest. "I drew little pink hearts—"

"Next to all your lines!" George finished

14

the sentence. "We know! We know!"

Nancy looked at her watch. They had been in the schoolyard fifteen minutes. It was time to go home.

As the girls walked out of the schoolyard they discussed the play.

"I hope I make a good Cheshire Cat," Nancy told her friends.

"Don't worry," Bess giggled. "You'll be purrfect!"

"In that direction lives a Hatter," Nancy said as the Cheshire Cat. She put down her cookie to point. "And in that direction lives a March Hare!"

"Don't forget to grin!" Hannah Gruen said. Hannah was the Drew's housekeeper, and she was helping Nancy practice her lines. Hannah had taken care of Nancy since she was three years old. That's when Nancy's mother had died.

"Hannah!" Nancy groaned. "I'm running out of funny jokes to think about!"

"This should make you smile," Hannah said. She held up the Cheshire Cat costume she had been sewing for Nancy.

Nancy flashed a big smile. The cat costume looked like fuzzy, orange pajamas. Hannah had also made a matching headband with pointy little cat ears.

"All it needs is a tail," Hannah said. "But I'm working at it."

"Thanks, Hannah!" Nancy said. "That costume is as neat as . . . as Orson's hat!"

The phone rang. Hannah's hands were full, so Nancy ran to answer it.

"Hello?" Nancy asked.

"Nancy!" a boy's voice hissed over the phone. "It's me, Orson!"

"Orson?" Nancy asked, surprised. She gave Hannah a curious look. Why was Orson calling her?

"You've got to help me, Nancy," Orson said in a shaky voice. "You've got to!"

"Why? What's wrong?" Nancy asked. She had never heard Orson sound so worried.

"Someone stole my hat!" Orson wailed. "That's what's wrong!"

3

Gadgets and Gizmos

Are you sure it's been stolen?" Nancy asked.

"Positive!" Orson said. "I left the hat by a tree while I played kickball. When I went back for it, it was gone!"

Tree? Nancy suddenly remembered Kyle. And the way he sneaked around Orson's hat.

"Nancy, I need that hat!" Orson cried. "Without it, I can't remember my lines. It's practically magic!"

Magic? Nancy thought. She tried hard not to giggle.

"Will you help solve the case, Detective Drew?" Orson asked.

Nancy gulped. She usually liked helping people. Unless they were pests—like Orson!

"Can I think about it?" Nancy asked.

"Okay," Orson groaned. "But don't think too long. We've got a situation!"

Nancy heard a click. Orson had hung up.

"What did Orson want?" Hannah asked.

"The Mad Hatter has a new riddle," Nancy sighed. "What's red, green, and yellow polka-dotted? And *missing*?"

"Don't forget to come to my party on Saturday, Phoebe!" Brenda announced in the auditorium the next morning. "You too, Jenny. And you, Emily. Don't forget!"

Nancy watched as Brenda handed out more bright pink invitations.

"Does she have to say it so loud?" Bess whispered.

"That's the idea!" George whispered back. "She wants to remind us that we were uninvited! Right, Nancy?"

"Sure," Nancy said. But she wasn't thinking about Brenda's party. She was too busy thinking about Orson's phone call.

"Okay, boys and girls!" Mrs. Reynolds called out. "Today we're going to rehearse the Mad Hatter's tea party again."

Orson walked up onto the stage.

"Where's your great, big, wonderful hat, Orson?" Mrs. Reynolds asked.

"M-My hat?" Orson stammered. "Um . . . it gives me hat hair. I'll wear it the day of the play."

Snickers filled the auditorium.

"Since when does Orson care about his hair?" Bess asked.

"Since his hat disappeared," Nancy explained.

"You mean his hat is missing?" George gasped. "No way!"

Mrs. Reynolds' class began rehearsing the play. Everyone knew their lines except Orson.

"The play is next Friday, Orson," Mrs. Reynolds said. "If you can't remember your lines, someone else will have to play the Mad Hatter."

"Someone else?" Orson cried. His shoulders dropped. "Yes, Mrs. Reynolds."

For the first time Nancy felt sorry for Orson. So after Mrs. Reynolds called a break, Nancy told him she would help.

"Neato-mosquito!" Orson cheered. He grabbed Nancy's hand and pumped it. "We'll make an awesome team!"

"Team?" Nancy asked, grabbing her hand back. "Bess and George always help me with my cases."

"Always!" Bess and George said over Nancy's shoulder.

"Ha!" Orson laughed. "Do Bess and George just happen to have a secret spy kit? Filled with the latest crime-solving gadgets and gizmos?"

"A what?" Nancy cried.

Orson ran to his seat. He reached under it and pulled out a colorful canvas bag. "I couldn't wait to use this!" he declared. "Now's my big chance!"

Bess and George shook their heads.

"Sorry, Nancy," George whispered. "But if Orson works on this case, I won't."

"Me, neither!" Bess said. "He's too much of a pest."

"I heard that!" Orson snapped. "And Nancy doesn't need your help, anyway!"

"Yes, I do!" Nancy blurted.

"So you won't work on this case without us, right?" George asked Nancy.

Nancy stared at her friends. How could she tell them that she *had* to?

"I promised Orson I would help," Nancy said. "And a promise is a promise."

"You heard her," Orson said. "A deal's a deal. So deal with it!"

"Fine," George said.

"Good luck," Bess said.

Nancy watched as her two best friends walked away. She felt awful!

"Well, what are we waiting for?" Orson asked Nancy. "Let's get to work!"

"Okay," Nancy said. "But first let me take out my detective notebook."

"What's that?" Orson asked.

"It's where I write down all my suspects and clues," Nancy answered.

"What are they?" Orson asked.

Nancy sighed. Working with Orson wasn't going to be easy. She pulled out her notebook and turned to a clean page.

"Here!" Orson said. He held out a bright green-and-orange pen. "Use this!"

"It's a nice pen," Nancy admitted. "But why should I use it?"

"Teamwork!" Orson replied. He shook the pen at Nancy. "Go ahead. It's yours."

"Thanks." Nancy shrugged. She took the pen and wrote "The Mystery of the Missing Hat" at the top of the page.

"Nancy and *Orson's* Mystery of the Missing Hat!" Orson corrected.

Nancy groaned to herself as she changed the words. Then on the same page she drew a sketch of Orson's missing hat.

"There was a label inside," Orson reminded her. "It said, 'Sid's Novelty Shop.'"

Nancy drew the label under the picture of the hat. Then she began her list of suspects.

"My first suspect is Kyle," Nancy said. "He was mad at you for knocking into him with your big hat. And I saw him sneaking around your hat in the schoolyard yesterday."

Orson's jaw dropped open. "Then case

closed!" he declared. "Kyle stole my hat—and that's that!"

"No, the case is not closed," Nancy said, shaking her head. "We still need more proof!"

"Rats!" Orson muttered. Then his eyes lit up. "Hey! That Troy Marvello wanted my hat—for his store window. Remember?"

"Yes," Nancy agreed. "But I didn't see Troy in the schoolyard yesterday."

"Then who else?" Orson asked.

Nancy glanced around the auditorium. Most of the kids were sitting quietly and reading their scripts. But Brenda was busy passing out more party invitations.

"Hmm," Nancy thought out loud. "Brenda said your hat was *perfect*."

"So?" Orson asked.

"She's also having a party," Nancy said. "Where everybody has to wear something special."

"*So?*" Orson asked again.

"So," Nancy said slowly, "maybe that something special is . . . a *hat*!"

4

Queen Brenda's Surprise

A hat party?" Orson asked. "How would we know for sure?"

Nancy noticed a bunch of backpacks piled up against the wall. One had a bright pink envelope sticking out of its pocket.

"That's Emily's backpack," Nancy whispered. "And she has an invitation!"

"And the invitation must say what kind of a party it is!" Orson said. "Emily is onstage rehearsing. Let's grab her invitation and check it out!"

"It's not right to take things out of other

people's backpacks," Nancy said. "I'll ask Emily about it after school."

"Boring!" Orson groaned. He reached into his detective kit and pulled out a glove. "Let my Spy Smart Sticky Fingers do the trick!"

Orson crept over to Emily's backpack. When he reached for the invitation, it stuck to his fingertips!

"Let's see Bess and George do that!" Orson said, holding out the invitation.

Nancy read it quickly. "It's a Hats-Off-to-Brenda party!" she gasped. "And a prize will be given for the best hat!"

"No wonder Brenda wanted my hat!" Orson said. "We have to go to that party!"

"But how can we?" Nancy asked. "We never got invitations!"

"But we *do* have disguises!" Orson said sneakily. "My secret spy kit comes with two camouflage hats!"

Nancy didn't want to sneak into the party. But the sooner they found the hat, the sooner she'd stop working with Orson!

"Okay. Brenda's party is on Saturday." Nancy sighed. "Tomorrow is Saturday. I'll ring your doorbell at two o'clock."

"Teamwork!" Orson cheered. He grabbed Nancy's hand to shake.

"Ouch!" Nancy complained. Orson was still wearing his sticky fingers glove!

I promised to help, Nancy thought glumly. *And a promise is a promise!*

That night during dinner Nancy told her father about the missing hat. Mr. Drew was a lawyer. He often helped Nancy with her cases.

"Orson wants to use all these gadgets, Daddy!" Nancy complained.

Mr. Drew smiled as he poured dressing on his salad. "The most important things a detective can use, Pudding Pie," he said, "are her eyes and her ears!"

"And her mouth!" Hannah joked. "So she can eat a second helping of macaroni!"

Nancy smiled and held out her plate. "Yes, please!" she said.

Macaroni and cheese always made Nancy feel better. So why didn't she feel better about this case?

"Ta-daaaa!" Orson sang as he flung the door open.

It was Saturday afternoon. Nancy stood on Orson's doorstep with wide eyes.

"*That* is the weirdest-looking hat I have ever seen in my life!" Nancy gasped.

"Thanks!" Orson said cheerily. The big hat covered half of his face. There were holes cut out for his eyes and mouth. And a big spinning propeller on the top!

"Your turn!" Orson said. He plopped a huge hat over Nancy's head. A thick veil covered her face. A huge yellow sunflower bobbed on the top!

"It's called undercover work!" Orson said happily.

I wish I were *under the covers,* Nancy thought glumly. *At home—in bed!*

As they walked to Brenda's house, Nancy was worried. What if the Carlton's recognized her—or Orson? When Mrs. Carlton opened the front door she smiled.

"What clever hats!" Mrs. Carlton said. She waved them inside. "Brenda's party is downstairs in the basement."

"All systems go!" Orson hissed as they hurried downstairs.

Nancy looked around. The basement was decorated with balloons and streams of pink-and-white crepe paper. A big banner over the snack table read, LONG LIVE QUEEN BRENDA!

"Oh, great!" Orson sneered. "This party is all *girls*!"

Orson was right. Through her veil Nancy saw many girls from her class. Then she saw Brenda. She wore a blue velvet dress and a huge top hat decorated with big paper daisies.

"That's my hat!" Orson whispered. "And she ruined it with goofy flowers!"

Nancy and Orson froze as Brenda clapped her hands for attention.

"Hold onto your hats!" Brenda announced. "Because it's limbo time!"

Brenda turned on her CD player. Music filled the basement as Molly and Amara held up the long limbo bar. Girls giggled as they leaned backward under it.

"Whatever you do, Orson," Nancy whispered, "do not lose your hat!"

When it was Nancy's turn she slid under the limbo bar. But when Orson went under the bar he froze.

Nancy froze too. The propeller on his hat was caught on the limbo bar!

"Okay, okay!" Brenda sighed. "What's the problem?"

"His—her hat is stuck on the limbo bar!" Nancy said, disguising her voice.

"Hel-lo?" Amara said, rolling her eyes. "Then take off the hat!"

"Take off the hat!" everyone chanted. "Take off the hat! Take off the hat!"

Oh, no! Nancy thought. *If Orson takes off his disguise, the truth will be out!*

Then Amara and Molly lifted the limbo bar—and lifted Orson's hat right off his head!

"It's Orson!" the girls shrieked.

"Busted!" Orson groaned.

"How did you get in here, Orson Wong?" Brenda demanded.

"He came with me!" Nancy said. She

stepped forward and pulled off her hat. "We were looking for his missing hat."

"We thought you stole it!" Orson said. He pointed to Brenda's top hat.

"Did not!" Brenda told Nancy. "My mother made this hat. I told her what Orson's hat looked like and she sewed one just like it—with flowers!"

Nancy was starting to believe Brenda. But Orson shook his head.

"Nice try, Carlton!" he sneered. "Now let's see what you're hiding under those daisies!"

Brenda shrieked as Orson plucked the daisies right off of her hat.

Suddenly Nancy noticed something. The hatband wasn't covered with yellow polka dots. It was covered with red stripes!

"Orson!" Nancy shouted. "Look at the hatband. It is not your hat!"

Orson stared at the hat. "Whoops." He gulped.

"Sorry, Brenda!" Nancy blurted. "We really didn't mean to—"

"Out!" Brenda shouted. She pointed to the door. "O-U-T—out!!"

The girls waved good-bye to Nancy as she and Orson hurried out of the basement.

"How could you do that?" Nancy demanded when they were both outside.

"I got us in, didn't I?" Orson asked.

They tossed their hats into a trash can. Then Nancy used Orson's pen to cross Brenda's name from her notebook.

"Now what do we do?" Nancy asked.

"Let's get some pizza!" Orson said. "We couldn't eat any chips or pretzels through those dumb hats!"

Nancy frowned. How could Orson think of food at a time like this?

But as they passed Casey's Department Store, they skidded to a stop.

Troy Marvello was in the window dressing a dummy. The dummy wore a long dress and a big hat. The hat had a red brim and a yellow polka-dotted hatband!

"Look, Orson!" Nancy gasped. "That hat looks just like yours!"

5

The Dress Mess

T hat *is* my hat!" Orson cried.

Troy didn't seem to notice Nancy or Orson. He was too busy working.

Nancy pulled out her notebook. She compared the hat in the window to her sketch. The two hats *looked* exactly the same. But were they the same?

"We have to get inside that window," Nancy said, "and see if that hat has a Sid's Novelty Store tag on it."

Nancy and Orson walked into the department store. The salespeople were busy helping customers.

"Which way to the window?" Nancy wondered out loud.

Suddenly she saw Troy. He was stepping out from behind a red curtain.

Nancy and Orson waited until Troy walked away. Then they quickly slipped behind the curtain.

"I can't believe it!" Orson whispered. "I'm inside a real store window."

Orson flattened his nose against the glass. People walking by looked up at him curiously.

"Will you stop?" Nancy cried. "Let's check out the hat and get out of here!"

"Wait!" Orson said. He reached into his pocket and plucked out a rubber dog nose. "Not until I put on my Secret Spy Schnozola!"

"What does *that* do?" Nancy asked.

"It's supposed to give me a keen sense of smell," Orson explained. "Just like a scent hound!"

"Whatever!" Nancy sighed.

Orson slipped on the nose and Nancy stood on her toes. She picked up the brim of the hat and read the label.

"Madame Colette's," Nancy read out loud. "That's not where you bought your—"

"I'll be in my window for a few minutes, Sally!" a voice interrupted.

Nancy gasped. It was Troy's voice. And he was coming back to the window!

"We have to hide!" Nancy whispered.

"Follow me!" Orson said. He tugged Nancy's arm and yanked her underneath the dummy's long, puffy skirt.

Nancy peeked out from under the skirt. She could see Troy's shoes right in front of her nose!

"What's a spring window?" Troy was asking himself, "without spring flowers?"

Nancy watched as red rose petals scattered on the floor.

"Roses make me sneeze!" Orson hissed. "And my Schnozola is making it worse!"

"Then take it off!" Nancy whispered back.

It was too late. "Ahh . . . ahh . . . choo!" Orson sneezed. He sneezed so hard that the long skirt blew out just enough to show Orson and Nancy's shoes.

"You two!" Troy shouted, lifting up the skirt. He was holding a basket of rose petals. "What are you doing under there?"

Nancy crawled out with Orson. She knew she would have to tell the truth.

"Orson's hat is missing," Nancy said. "And the dummy's hat looks just like his."

"It doesn't take a dummy to see that, Marvello!" Orson declared.

Troy folded his arms. "Impossible!" He laughed. "This hat was imported from a very expensive design house in Paris!"

Nancy remembered the label under the hat. The name of the store *did* sound French.

"That's why I wanted Orson's hat," Troy went on. "It looked just like the expensive kind."

"So you ordered the hat all the way from Paris?" Nancy asked.

"Yes," Troy said. He pulled the receipt from his pocket and held it up. "And it cost me over one hundred dollars."

"Bummer," Orson said. "Mine just cost seven dollars and fifty cents."

Nancy studied the receipt. Everything

Troy said was true. "I'm sorry if we caused any trouble," she said.

"And I'm sorry I didn't give you my hat," Orson admitted. "I didn't know you wanted it that badly!"

"It's okay," Troy smiled. "You gave me the idea. And that's also important."

Nancy smiled too. Until Orson threw back his head and started to sneeze . . .

"Ahh . . . ahh . . . choooo!"

Poof! Orson's sneeze blew a blast of rose petals into Troy's face.

Nancy and Orson raced out of the store.

"It's good that he wasn't very angry," Nancy told Orson.

"But *bad* that it wasn't my hat!" Orson sighed. "Now what do we do?"

They were about to walk along Main Street when Nancy spotted Lonny and Lenny.

"Hey, Lenny!" Orson called. "Why are you carrying your backpack on a Saturday?"

The twins stopped walking.

"Um," Lonny blurted. "We're coming from the magic shop."

"Yeah!" Lenny said. He nodded toward his backpack. "I just got an awesome trick card deck."

"Really?" Nancy asked. "May we see?"

"No!" Lonny blurted. He put his hands over Lenny's backpack.

"Leave us alone!" Lenny shouted.

Nancy stared at the twins. Why were they acting so weird? And what were they hiding inside that backpack?

6
Hypno-Tease

Lonny and Lenny turned and scurried up Main Street.

"Did you see the way Lenny guarded his backpack?" Nancy asked. "Do you think they might know something about the hat?"

Orson shook his head.

"Lonny and Lenny are pests but they're not thieves," he insisted. "And I didn't see them anywhere near my hat when it disappeared."

Nancy agreed. The only place Nancy saw the twins were behind the bushes, eating gummy worms.

Nancy pulled out her notebook and crossed out Troy's name. "Now our only suspect is—"

"Kyle!" Orson whispered. With wide eyes he pointed over Nancy's shoulder.

Nancy spun around. She saw Kyle Leddington standing in front of the Sweet Dreams Candy Store. He was sharing a big bag of candy with his friend, Peter.

"There's our man!" Orson sneered. "Kyle Leddington—our final suspect!"

"We don't know yet," Nancy warned. "We still need more evidence."

"You look for it," Orson said. "I'm going home for milk and cookies."

Nancy and Orson planned to meet the next day to look for clues. But before Orson left he tossed Nancy a pair of goofy-looking fake ears.

"They're my Secret Spy Hear-ears," Orson said as he walked away. "They'll let you hear things from miles and miles away!"

Nancy giggled as she tried on the silly fake ears. But then she heard something.

It was Kyle's voice coming in loud and clear! Could Orson's spy ears really work?

"That Orson won't be bothering me again," Kyle was saying.

"How come?" Peter asked.

"Because," Kyle said sneakily. "I took something that belonged to him!"

Nancy gasped. She couldn't believe her ears . . . her secret spy ears!

"So what are we going to do today?" Orson asked Nancy.

It was Sunday morning. Orson was standing on the Drew's doorstep. Draped over his shoulder was his secret spy bag.

"We're going to investigate Kyle," Nancy said. "I heard him tell Peter that he took something of yours."

"Aha!" Orson cried. He pumped his fist in the air. "I knew it! I knew it!"

Nancy made sure her detective notebook was in her jacket pocket. After saying good-bye to her father and Hannah she stepped outside and closed the door.

"First we have to go to Kyle's house,"

Nancy explained. "And then we have to question him."

"Bor-ring!" Orson groaned.

Nancy planted her hands on her hips. "Do you have a better idea?" she asked.

"You bet I do!" Orson said. He pulled out a plastic pair of goggles with whirly spirals on the lenses. "I say we hypnotize Kyle. And make him confess!"

Nancy stared at the glasses. They looked like something she would wear on Halloween!

"Well?" Orson asked. He put on the glasses and waved his fingers. "Are you getting sleepy?"

"Come on," Nancy said, rolling her eyes.

Nancy and Orson walked four blocks to the Leddington house. When Nancy rang the doorbell Mrs. Leddington opened the door.

"Kyle is upstairs in his room," she said. "I'm sure he'd love some company!"

Nancy and Orson climbed the stairs to Kyle's room. Kyle was sitting on his bed and playing an electronic game.

"What's up?" Kyle asked.

"Hi, Kyle," Nancy said. "We're looking for Orson's missing hat. Do you know where it is?"

"In other words," Orson sneered, "where did you stash it, Leddington?"

Kyle stood up. "I didn't steal your dumb hat!" he insisted.

Orson pulled on the hypno-glasses. "Look into my eyes and tell me that," he said. "Deep . . . deep . . . deep into my eyes!"

"Orson!" Nancy complained. "Will you please get real?"

But Kyle was staring at Orson's goggles. His eyes were getting droopy.

"I'm . . . getting . . . sleepy," Kyle said.

No way! Nancy thought. But then again, Orson's fake ears seemed to work!

"Okay, March Hare," Orson said. "What did you do with my hat?"

Kyle kept staring at the goggles. "March Hare," he mumbled. "Hare . . . hare . . ."

Kyle jumped onto the bed. He began hopping up and down. "Boing! Boing! Boing!" he shouted.

"What's he doing?" Nancy asked as Kyle hopped around the room.

"He's hypnotized." Orson shrugged. "And he thinks he's a rabbit."

Nancy stared at Kyle. He was wiggling his nose like a rabbit too!

"Can't you de-hypnotize him?" Nancy cried as Kyle hopped past her.

"We have to catch him first!" Orson said.

Nancy and Orson chased Kyle around the room. All of a sudden Kyle stopped hopping. He pulled a Squishy, Squirty Head out of his pocket.

"Made you look!" Kyle laughed as he squirted Orson and Nancy.

"Aaahhhh!" Nancy and Orson yelled.

Dripping wet, Nancy glared at Kyle. "You tricked us!" she scolded.

"Sure," Kyle chuckled. "You didn't really think I fell for those dorky glasses, did you?"

Orson stepped up to Kyle.

"That's *my* Squishy, Squirty Head!" he said. "I was so busy looking for my hat—I didn't even know it was gone!"

So! Nancy thought. *Kyle took Orson's*

Squishy, Squirty Head, not his hat!

"When did you take it?" Orson demanded.

"Last Thursday in the schoolyard," Kyle shrugged. "When you were playing kickball I snatched it from your backpack."

"No wonder I saw you sneaking around Orson's backpack!" Nancy told Kyle.

"Great," Orson groaned. He began stuffing his hypno-glasses in his spy kit. "That was my favorite Squishy, Squirty Head!"

"Wait!" Kyle said. He pointed to Orson's bag. "Is that a secret spy kit?"

Orson nodded.

"Does it come with the Secret Spy Vanishing Ink Pen?" Kyle asked excitedly.

"Yeah," Orson said. "But I gave it to Nancy to use on her case."

Nancy's mouth dropped open. Orson's pen had vanishing ink?

"What?" Nancy cried. She opened her notebook and let out a gasp. The pages of her case were totally blank!

Oh, no! Nancy thought. *My Mystery of the Missing Hat—is missing!*

7

The Last Straw

Awesome!" Orson cheered. "The ink really *does* disappear."

Orson and Kyle gave each other a high five. But Nancy was mad.

"You tricked me!" Nancy scolded Orson. "You gave me that pen on purpose!"

"I just wanted to see if it worked," Orson said. "I guess it does!"

"How about a switch?" Kyle asked. "The pen for your Squishy, Squirty Head!"

"Deal!" Orson said.

The boys made the switch. Then Nancy and Orson left Kyle's house.

"You shouldn't have given me that pen, Orson," Nancy said angrily. "My detective notebook is important to me."

"So is my hat," Orson said. "And you should have solved this case by now!"

"Me?" Nancy cried. "What about team-work?"

"I know!" Orson groaned. "But if I don't know my lines by Tuesday I'll be the *Sad Hatter.*"

Nancy was worried too. They had no more suspects. And time was running out.

"We've got the whole afternoon to look for more clues," Orson said. "So let's go for it."

"Can't," Nancy said. "Hannah wants me to try on my Cheshire Cat costume."

"What?" Orson cried.

Nancy tried to calm Orson down. "To-morrow is Monday," she said. "We can search the schoolyard and the auditorium for more clues—"

"Tomorrow is too late!" Orson muttered. "We have to do something now!"

As Orson stormed off, Nancy opened her

notebook. She hoped that maybe the ink had reappeared.

No such luck. The pages were still blank.

"Bess and George would never do this," Nancy said with a sigh. "Not in a million years."

Nancy walked straight home. After eating a chicken salad sandwich she tried on her Cheshire Cat costume.

"All it needed was a tail," Hannah asked. "What do you think?"

Nancy wiggled the tail in front of the full-length mirror. It was the perfect touch to a perfect costume!

"I love it!" Nancy exclaimed.

Her puppy, Chocolate Chip, looked up at Nancy and wagged her tail.

"Even Chip likes it," Hannah said. "Why don't you show your dad?"

"Okay!" Nancy said happily.

But on her way to the living room Nancy heard the doorbell. She climbed onto a step stool, and looked through the peephole.

"Oh, great," Nancy groaned. It was Orson Wong!

"Open the door," Orson urged. "I have something to help us with the case."

Nancy rolled her eyes. "Is it something from your spy kit again?"

"No!" Orson said. "Something better!"

Chocolate Chip ran over to Nancy. She began whining and scratching at the door.

What does Orson have? Nancy wondered. She jumped off the stool and opened the door. "Stay, Chip," Nancy told her dog. Then she stepped outside.

"Cool cat costume," Orson said.

"Thanks," Nancy said. "What do you want to show me?"

Orson stuck two fingers into his mouth and gave a loud whistle. A basset hound with long, floppy ears ran out from under the picnic table.

"Meet my neighbor's dog, Hubert," Orson explained. "Every detective needs a good scent hound."

"Why a scent hound?" Nancy cried.

"To sniff out clues!" Orson answered.

Hubert cocked his head as he looked at Nancy. Then he let out a long whine.

"Uh-oh," Orson gulped. "I don't think Hubert likes cats."

"But I'm not really a—"

Hubert barked. He kicked up his legs and began chasing Nancy around the yard!

"Orson!" Nancy shouted as she and Hubert ran around the picnic table. "Call off your dog!"

"He's not *my* dog!" Orson shrugged.

Nancy jumped up onto the picnic bench. But when she looked down she groaned. Hubert had her cat's tail between his paws!

"Look what that dog did!" Nancy complained. "He pulled off my tail!"

Orson smiled as Hubert chewed up the fuzzy orange cat's tail. "Hubert rules!" he exclaimed. "Think of what he'll do when he finds the hat thief!"

Nancy gritted her teeth. She felt her cheeks beginning to burn.

"That does it!" Nancy snapped. "So far you've been nasty to our suspects. You played a mean trick on me. And you don't even care that my costume is ruined!"

"What's your point?" Orson asked.

"My point is," Nancy said slowly. "I'm not working on this case anymore."

"You can't drop this case!" Orson gasped. "We're a team. You even wrote it in your notebook!"

"It disappeared!" Nancy snapped. "Remember?"

Orson heaved a big sigh. He grabbed Hubert's leash and left the yard.

Nancy picked up the shredded cat's tail. She felt bad too. But not just because of the tail. She had never dropped a case before. Ever!

"What kind of detective am I?" Nancy asked Bess and George the next day. "Good detectives always stick to their cases."

The three friends carried their trays down the lunch line.

"You *are* a good detective, Nancy!" Bess said. "The best!"

"Thanks." Nancy sighed. She slid her tray along the counter. "But I'll never find the missing hat now."

George grabbed a container of milk and

smiled. "Who says you won't?" she asked. "All you need is the right team!"

"Team?" Nancy asked.

Bess nodded. "Me, you, and George!" Nancy smiled from ear to ear. Not only was she back on the case, she was back with her two best friends!

"We'll have to start from scratch," Nancy said. "With new suspects and clues."

The girls inched their way down the lunch line. They smiled at a bulletin board covered with colorful collages.

"There's an ice-cream sundae made out of cotton and buttons!" Bess pointed out.

"And a polka-dotted banana!" George giggled.

Nancy glanced at the banana. Her eyes flew wide open. "Hey!" she said. "That looks like the same polka-dotted material from Orson's hatband!"

"Who made it?" George asked.

Nancy peered at the name in the corner of the collage. "Omigosh!" she gasped. "It's made by Lenny Wong!"

8

Nancy Takes a Bow

Do you think Lonny and Lenny stole the hat?" Bess asked Nancy.

"They were acting weird when Orson and I saw them the other day," Nancy admitted. "But they weren't near the hat when it disappeared."

"Yeah," George agreed. "They were behind the bushes eating gummy worms."

"Let's search the schoolyard after school," Nancy suggested. "Maybe we can find more clues."

"Are you going to write the twins' names in your notebook?" Bess asked.

"Yes," Nancy said. "But this time I'm using my own pen!"

At three o'clock the girls hurried to the schoolyard. Molly, Amara, and Emily invited them to jump rope but they had work to do.

Nancy, Bess, and George ran to the tree where the hat was last seen. They searched the ground for clues.

"Nothing!" Nancy sighed.

"Maybe the hat wasn't stolen," George said slowly.

"What do you mean?" Nancy asked.

"Remember the wind that blew away Bess's script?" George asked. "Maybe it blew Orson's hat away too."

Nancy's eyes lit up.

"Good idea, George!" Nancy said. "But which way would the hat have blown?"

"The wind blew my script over the bushes," Bess pointed out.

The girls squeezed through the bushes and walked around. There was no hat.

Nancy looked closer. Carefully she parted a few bushes with her hands.

That's when Nancy found it. Stuck between two bushes was a bright red swatch of material.

"It's the same color as the hat's brim," Nancy said. "But where is the rest of the hat?"

"I found something too!" George said. She held up two candy gummy worms. "Looks like Lonny and Lenny left a little trail!"

"Busted!" a voice whispered.

The girls whirled around. Lonny and Lenny were just ducking behind the bushes.

"Hey!" George shouted.

Nancy, Bess, and George looked over the bushes. The twins were running away.

"Wait!" Nancy shouted. "We want to ask you something!"

Nancy and her friends squeezed through the bushes. They began chasing the twins throughout the schoolyard.

"Freeze!" Bess called. "Like a popsicle!"

But Lonny and Lenny kept darting around swings, monkey bars, and seesaws. Then they tried to race through Molly and Amara's jump rope. . . .

"Help!" the twins shouted.

Nancy stopped running. The twins were tangled in the twisted rope!

"Now look what you did!" Emily snapped at the twins. "I was already up to 'S my name is Susan'!"

"Get us out of here!" Lonny cried.

"We will," Nancy said sternly, "when you tell us if you have Orson's hat."

"Okay!" Lonny said. "The answer is yes— and no!"

"What does that mean?" Nancy asked.

"Remember when we found Bess's script behind the bushes?" Lenny asked.

"After you left we also found the hat," Lenny added.

"We knew it was Orson's," Lonny went on. "All we wanted to do was borrow it so we could pull a rabbit out of a hat."

"So we took the hat to Timmy's house!" Lenny said. "But when we put his rabbit inside he kicked holes in the hat!"

Lenny reached into his backpack. He pulled out a hat full of holes.

"See?" Lenny said. "Swiss cheese!"

Nancy stared at the tattered hat. "That's Orson's hat!" she gasped.

"Why didn't you tell Orson?" Bess asked the twins.

"We were scared that he would pour oatmeal in our slippers!" Lenny shuddered. "He does that when he's mad!"

"So we hid it!" Lonny said. "Except when I needed it for my collage. It was torn anyway."

Amara and Molly rolled their eyes.

"Three pests in one family!" Amara sighed. "How do you think *that* happened?"

Lenny strained against the jump rope. "You're not going to tell Orson, are you?" he asked Nancy.

"It's *your* job to tell him," Nancy said. "And if you don't, I'll tell your mom that you were eating gummy worms after school!"

"Oh, man!" the twins groaned.

"Okay, that's it," Molly said. She started to untangle the twins. "We want our jump rope back."

Nancy, Bess, and George left the schoolyard and began walking home.

"I'm happy we solved this case," Nancy admitted. "But Orson still won't be able to wear his hat."

"Which means he won't remember his lines either." Bess sighed. "Maybe the hat *was* magic!"

The girls walked past Brenda Carlton's house. Nancy saw Brenda jamming something into the trashcan.

"Hi, Brenda," Nancy said. "What are you throwing away?"

"The hat I wore on Saturday!" Brenda answered. "It didn't even win me first prize. Not even at my own party!"

Brenda clanged the trash can shut. Then she stomped into her house.

Nancy carefully reached into the trash can and pulled out the hat. Then she yanked off some of the daisies.

"Look!" she said. "Underneath it really *does* look like Orson's hat!"

George plucked off the hatband. "Now it *really* looks like Orson's hat!"

"Let's give this hat to Orson!" Nancy said. "He'll know it's not his real hat—but maybe he'll give this one a chance."

Nancy carried the hat home. The next morning she brought the hat to school and into the auditorium.

"My hat!" Orson cried. "You found my hat just in time!"

Before Nancy could explain, Orson grabbed the hat. He plopped it onto his head and began babbling his lines.

Nancy didn't get it. Didn't the twins tell Orson about his real hat?

"The Mad Hatter is back!" Orson cheered. "And better than ever!"

While Orson ran over to Mrs. Reynolds, Nancy turned to her friends.

"Orson thinks I found his real hat!" Nancy said. "Which means the twins still didn't tell him the truth."

"Let's hope they don't tell him until *after* the play on Friday!" George said.

"Yeah." Bess giggled. "Orson may be a pest, but he's a pretty good Mad Hatter!"

Nancy smiled to herself. The hat was never magic. Orson just *thought* it was!

****

On Friday the curtain came up on *Alice in Wonderland*. George blew too many bubbles from her bubble pipe. And Kyle knocked over the teapot. But everyone remembered their lines. And Nancy didn't forget to grin once!

When the play was over, Mrs. Reynolds' class joined hands and bowed. Other students and families cheered. *Alice in Wonderland* was a big hit!

"I'm sad that the play is over," Bess whispered as they kept on bowing.

"Me too," George whispered.

"Me three!" Nancy giggled.

But Nancy still had work to do. So that night she sat on her bed and opened her notebook. Then she began to write. . . .

"Daddy gave me pink roses after the play. He also gave me advice that really clicked. A good detective doesn't need gadgets and gizmos to solve a mystery. Just her eyes, her ears, and something else. Good friends like Bess and George. And *that* is something to grin about!"

Case Closed!

**Do your younger brothers and sisters
want to read books like yours?**

Let them know there are books just for *them!*"

They can join Nancy Drew and her best
friends as they collect clues and solve mysteries in

THE
NANCY DREW
NOTEBOOKS®

Starting with
#1 The Slumber Party Secret
#2 The Lost Locket
#3 The Secret Santa
#4 Bad Day for Ballet

AND

Meet up with suspense and mystery

in The Hardy Boys® are: The Clues Brothers™

Starting with
#1 The Gross Ghost Mystery
#2 The Karate Clue
#3 First Day, Worst Day
#4 Jump Shot Detectives

Look for a brand-new story every
other month at your local bookseller

Published by Simon & Schuster

2325